# A visit to City Farm

Verna Wilkins

Illustrated by Karin Littlewood

Firetree books

A VISIT TO CITY FARM
published by Firetree books, 2016
PO Box 61283, London N17 1DY

Text © Verna Wilkins
Illustrations © Karin Littlewood
The right of Verna Wilkins and Karin Littlewood to be identified as the author and illustrator
of this work has been asserted in accordance with the Copyright, Designs and Patents Acts 1988.

ISBN 978-1-911402-07-7

A CIP catalogue record for this book is available from the British Library.

Printed in China by Toppan Leefung

Supported using public funding by

ARTS COUNCIL
ENGLAND

LOTTERY FUNDED

MIX
Paper from
responsible sources
FSC® C104723
FSC
www.fsc.org

*This book was made for and with the children of*
*Chalkhill Primary School.*

Aadarsha
Aboo
Alaa
Alex
Alexandru
Amelia
Anamaria
Ariza
Arthur
Artur
Asheel
Benedicte
Bridget
Bruna
Charlotte
Denis

Emanuel
Farida
Gabriel
Garisha
Ghiyas
Glen
Ibrahim
Iimaan
Jade
Jamila
Janika
Julien
Kathey
Khatra
Kome
Kurie

Lina
Lionel
Mahmoud
Manyo
Mariam
Mazneen
Merlyn
Mudasir
Nadir
Nisha
Nuradin
Patryk
Reece
Riosha
Salma
Samira

Samira
Seddiq
Siddh
Tiago
Wiilo
Wyasion
Yohann
Younas
Yusuf
Zainab
Zakariya

Rainbow Class at Fernhill School was excited.
Everyone was happy.
Miss Jama and her class were getting ready
for their visit to City Farm.

"Are you ready, Rainbow Class?"
"Yes, Miss Jama."
"Are you ready, Salma?"
"Yes, Miss Jama. But Alex can't
remember what you told us
to remember."

"Can you tell us one thing we must remember, Salma?"

"Walk in pairs," said Salma.

"Very good."

"Hold hands and stay together," said Nadia.

"Excellent!"

"Oh! said Alex. "I can remember now… We must keep to the left along the road."

"Excellent Alex," said Miss Jama.

Mr Ricardo did his final check and Rainbow class set off.

Coats zipped,
Rucksacks light,
Hands free
For holding tight.

There was howling traffic along the road.
"Look! There's my grandma!" said Josh.
"She looks after the flowers."
"Hi Grandma!" said all his friends.
Grandma waved.

"Salma!" called Miss Jama. "Keep up."
Everybody marched into the station.

A noisy train came roaring
out of a deep, dark tunnel
and stopped.

"Everybody on!"
said the nice man
who helped them
onto the train.

They hustled and bustled
Till they all found a seat
And away they went
For a wonderful treat.

City Farm was ready for Rainbow Class.

Enormous goats with floppy ears,
Tiny ponies walking in pairs,
Squirrels scampering round and round
Over fences and on the ground.

Some sheep moved slowly and bleated loudly.
"This lot are as noisy as Rainbow Class!" said Miss Jama.

Fun facts

- Sheep eat plants, such as grass.
- Female sheep are called ewes.
- Male sheep are called rams.
- Baby sheep are called lambs.

An enormous pig in a messy sty,
Grunted and groaned as they crept by.
They were quiet and quick
as they hurried away.
Sleep well Mister Pig!
Have a nice day.

Suddenly
with a sound like thunder
a herd of horses came galloping to the fence.
TJ shrieked and ran away.

Mr Ricardo found him.
"Oh, there you are, TJ.
Let's find the others."

"It's feeding time for the horses," said the man from the farm.
"They are very hungry!" said TJ.
"Time for our lunch too!" said Miss Jama.

"I am so hungry!" said TJ.
"Me too!"

After lunch Rainbow Class went to meet the llamas.
"Llamas come from South America where they work
very hard," said Miss Jama. "Look at those eyelashes!"

"Are these llamas too?" asked Amanda.
"No, they are alpacas. They come from
South America too," said the man from the farm.
"Just feel their beautiful, soft coats."

"Why are the chickens fenced in?"
asked Josh.
"To keep them safe from foxes
that might eat them."
"I love chicken dinners.
But my mum cooks them first!"
"We don't eat meat!" said Nadia.
"Only vegetables."

"Look!" said Salma.
"That goose has lost his head!"
"Shoo!" shouted Alex.

Out popped the goose's head
from under its wing

and it scooted away.
Everyone laughed.

"Look at this bird! He's amazing. He must be off to a pheasant fancy dress party," said Mr Ricardo.

GOLDEN PHEASANT
from China

Too soon, it was time to leave City Farm.
Rainbow Class said goodbye to the animals.

Horses neighing,
Donkeys braying,
Cows mooing,
Llamas chewing.

"This was the best day ever," said
Rainbow Class.

# Chalkhill Primary School
## are the proud co-publishers of this book

Chalkhill Primary School is a popular 2-form-entry school in the London Borough of Brent. It is framed by the Wembley Stadium arch and located in a residential community of modern flats and houses. Brent has a rich cultural heritage due to traditional links with Commonwealth countries and more recently with countries joining the European Union. Eighty-five percent of the pupils have English as an additional language.

Wembley Park tube station nearby offers access to central London where theatres, museums and other places of interest provide wonderful educational experiences for our children. We also organise residential trips to outward bound centres in Hampshire and Kent. Pupils in Years 5 and 6 also undertake and enjoy an annual residential trip to Spain.

At Chalkhill Primary School, we aim to provide a safe, secure and healthy environment where all children are encouraged to be independent learners and thinkers. Through quality teaching and high expectations, we provide opportunities for our children to access an enriched and creative curriculum.

With this in mind, we were delighted to take on this amazing project: to make a picture book, *A visit to City Farm*. The children of Year 5 collaborated with the author, illustrator, editor and printer, in writing and publishing this beautiful book for Year 1 and Nursery children.

The Year 5 children were 'hands-on' from the idea to the finished product. This exciting venture helped them to develop a strong sense of identity and belonging, as well as taking responsibility for producing a book that will support younger readers in the school community.

Chalkhill has remained in the top ten schools in Brent over the last 3 years. OFSTED inspections in 2011 and in March 2016, confirm that Chalkhill continues to be a GOOD school. We are outstanding in Music and the first school in Brent to achieve the Gold Sing Up Award. We are also a Brent School Partnership Centre of Excellence for Early Years.

I am proud to be Head of Chalkhill Primary School and am grateful to the community and all stakeholders for their support.

*Rose Ashton*

Find more picture books at
# firetreebooks.co.uk